MW00906698

For Beret and Anna… still reading with Dad.
RLJ

For Cody and Lacey… the best of the best.
WDH

Jorgensen, Richard, 1946-
    Reading with Dad / written by Richard Jorgensen ; illustrated by Warren Hanson.
        p. cm.
    Summary: Reading together is a constant through the years in the relationship
between this loving father and daughter.
    ISBN 0-931674-41-7
    [1. Books and reading – Fiction. 2. Fathers and daughters – Fiction.
3. Stories in rhyme.] I. Hanson, Warren, ill. II. Title.
PZ8.3.J79 Re 2000
[E]–dc21   00-31943

Waldman House Press, Inc.
525 North Third Street
Minneapolis, Minnesota 55401

Reading With Dad

WRITTEN BY
RICHARD JORGENSEN
ILLUSTRATED BY
WARREN HANSON

WALDMAN HOUSE PRESS

MINNEAPOLIS

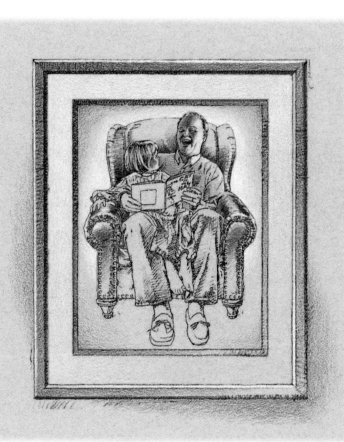

We're there in the photo that hangs on the wall,

the first childhood memory I can recall...

The three of us snug in the overstuffed chair —

(well, two — it just seems like the third one was there) —

The Cat In The Hat, my father, and I.

It's just before bed and I'm warm and I'm dry.

My father is laughing, I'm turning to look,

and I'm watching him laugh as he's reading the book.

We're having such fun, and he's holding me tight.

There was always a book before saying good-night.

That photograph shows the best times that I've had:

all of those times I spent reading with Dad.

When I was eight I could read by myself,

but sometimes the books would be left on the shelf

as dolls, pets, and teddy bears filled up that space

where storybook walls made a daydreaming place.

Still, my favorite time at the end of each day

was to sit by the fire, all my toys put away…

(well, most of them); then I would open a book,

knowing that Daddy would listen and look.

And there at the foot of the overstuffed chair

I would read to my dolly and hamster and bear.

They all loved the stories, but what made me feel glad

was that all of us really were reading with Dad.

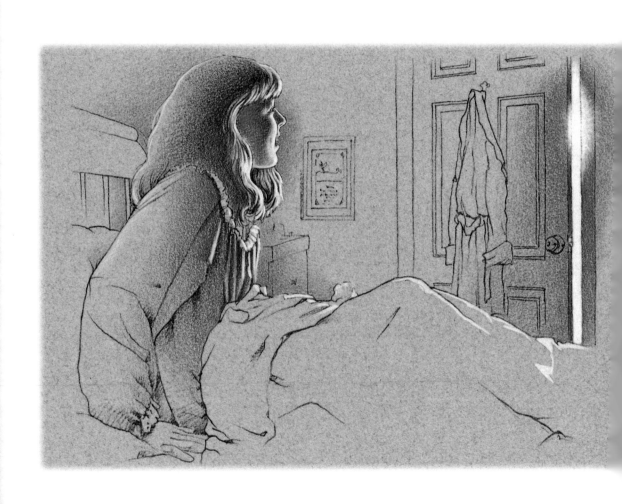

Then came a magical summertime night.

I was trying to sleep, but the moon was too bright,

when I heard my dad's footsteps from out in the hall —

he couldn't sleep either. So he whispered a call…

"Hey… you awake? Here, I've got just the thing —

let's go out to the porch and sit on the swing.

You grab the flashlight, I'll bring what we need

to send you to dreamland. Come on! Let's go read!"

Then night after night it was pirates and kings,

then Wind in the Willows, then wizards and rings —

Tale after tale from the books that he had,

but the greatest adventure was reading with Dad!

As I grew, all those stories and words had me hooked;

most evenings the library table was booked.

Though high school meant homework, athletics (and boys!),

the library's shelves held the greatest of joys:

Dickens and Austen and Brontë and Twain

were friends I would visit again and again.

Later, at college, each time I would call,

he'd ask, "What are you reading?" and want to know all

about what I was thinking of Shakespeare or Poe

or Homer or Wordsworth or Frost or Thoreau.

The long-distance bill must have looked pretty bad —

across all those miles I was reading with Dad.

Now the leather is cracked in the overstuffed chair, and it now sits in my house and is the place where I read to my children. They cuddle beside.

And though it is bedtime, their eyes open wide

as the pictures and poems and stories unfold

from inside the covers of books new and old.

And sometimes their grandpa will listen a while

as he sits by the fire, and I'll catch a faint smile

or a gleam in his eye as he gives me a wink,

a gleam that will cause me to quietly think

of what he is thinking…

the grand times that we've had.

After all of these years, I'm still reading with Dad.

Now he is the one who is lying in bed;

I fluff up the pillow beneath his gray head,

and I know that although he is ready to rest,

he wants me to read from the books we love best.

And so once again we fall under that spell

as we travel the story road we've known so well.

This story is short though — he's weary, I see,

so I quietly finish with Psalm Twenty-three.

Then softly, he says, as I turn out the light,

"There was always a book before saying good-night."

The best of the best times that I've ever had

are all of those times I've spent reading with Dad.